UnpOppable

tim hopgood

MACMILLAN CHILDREN'S BOOKS

"It's unpOPpable!" said the boy,

as he stood on his big yellow balloon.

"It's un**pOp**pable!" said the boy,

as it blew into the holly tree.

"It's un**pOp**pable!" said the boy,

as it danced along the aerials.

"It's **unstOppable!**" said the boy,

as it drifted up above the chimneys.

"Come back!" called the boy.

"Please don't go!"

But the yellow balloon didn't seem to hear.

"My unpoppable, it's disappeared," sniffed the boy.

But the balloon knew

where it was going!

Up and up it went.

Higher than the stars, around the moon, and all the way past . . .

... the
Milky Way.

And still it didn't go pOp.

What's that?

Wondered the boy.

"Is this yours?"

said a strange voice

from behind the big balloon.

"Yes!" said the boy, "it's my unpOOppable!"

"Well, thank you for sending it to find me," said the little spaceman.

"But this is no ordinary unpoppable"

"Are you

ready for

something

spectacular?"

Tim Hopgood lives in
York
North Yorkshire
ENGLAND
UK
Europe
NORTHERN HEMISPHERE
PLANET EARTH
THE SOLAR SYSTEM
KUIPER BELT
Oort Cloud
Orion Spur
MILKY WAY GALAXY
· · · · · · · · · · · · · · · · · · · ·
THE DARK UNIVERSE